Congratulations!

to

....

from

....

The text of this book is set in New Century Schoolbook and OPTI Majer Irregular.
The illustrations are watercolor and charcoal pencil, reproduced in full color.

Library of Congress Cataloging-in-Publication Data

Zoehfeld, Kathleen Weidner.
Curious you : on your way! / by Kathleen W. Zoehfeld ; illustrated by H. A. Rey.
p. cm.
Summary: Provides words of congratulations, encouragement, and love to a curious
monkey who has accomplished much, but still has many things to see, to do, and to dream.
ISBN-13: 978-0-618-91975-8 (hardcover)
[1. Self-esteem—Fiction. 2. Monkeys—Fiction.] I. Rey, H. A. (Hans Augusto),
1898–1977, ill. II. Title.
PZ7.Z715Cur 2008
[E]—dc22
2007012922

Manufactured in Singapore
TWP 10 9 8 7 6 5

Curious You
On Your Way!

Written by Kathleen W. Zoehfeld   Illustrated by H. A. Rey

HOUGHTON MIFFLIN COMPANY
BOSTON 2008

HIP, HIP, HOORAY!

You've done great things.

The whole world is proud of **YOU** today.

You've learned so much.
You studied hard.

And put your brains to the test.

You played on the team!

Of course, the time comes when
a curious monkey needs to *break free!*

Even if it means you don't know exactly
where you're going . . .

or what
will come next.

So much to **see!**

So much to **try!**

What should you **do?**

It's up to **YOU.**

Just **follow your dreams** and you'll soar.

You may feel
a little frightened
at times. But . . .
hold on tight!

You'll **see sights** that take your breath away!

You'll find the spot where you most want to land.

Oh, what a place it will be!

The thrill of discovery will be yours.

And if things don't work out quite as you had planned . . . **don't worry!**

All great explorers **bump** and **crash** sometimes.

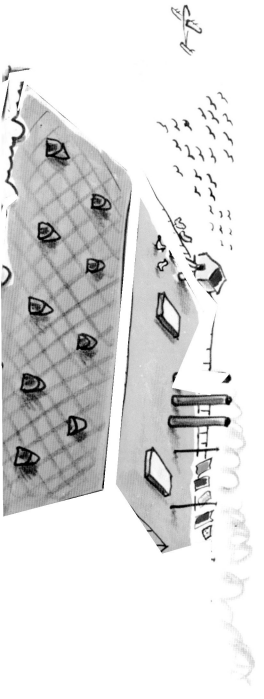

There will always be **new heights** to reach.

Whatever you do,
you will
find your own style.

Even if it **surprises** a few!

You'll **give to others** in ways that only **you** can.

And you will make **new friends.**

The world needs
you **now.**

You've got

BIG

ideas.

The feats you imagine
you'll just **HAVE** to try . . .
and imagination can lead to invention.

Before you know it,

the **SPOTLIGHT** will be on **YOU**.

What will your story be?
Bold and inspiring—
a tale of curiosity
and brave exploration!

Everyone will line up to see!

And if the path that you choose gets rocky and rough—

whenever you feel all alone—

remember,

we're with you all the way.
Today, tomorow . . .

. . . and every day!

We're proud of **curious YOU.**